## LONE STAR HEROINES

# MESSENGER
## on the
# BATTLEFIELD

### Melinda Rice

**Illustrations by Toni Thomas**

Other books in the Lone Star Heroines series:

*Fire on the Hillside*
by Melinda Rice

*Secrets in the Sky*
by Melinda Rice

The Lone Star Heroes series:

*Comanche Peace Pipe*
by Patrick Dearen

*On the Pecos Trail*
by Patrick Dearen

*The Hidden Treasure of the Chisos*
by Patrick Dearen

LONE STAR HEROINES

# MESSENGER
## on the
# BATTLEFIELD

**Melinda Rice**

Republic of Texas Press
Plano, Texas

**Library of Congress Cataloging-in-Publication Data**

Rice, Melinda.
    Messenger on the battlefield / Melinda Rice.
        p.  cm. — (Lone Star heroines)
    Summary: Eleven-year-old Isabel Montoya's family is divided when
    Texas goes to war against Mexico and they must decide whether to
    remain true to their heritage or fight for their new homeland.
    ISBN 1-55622-788-4 (pbk.)
    1. Texas—History—Revolution, 1835-1836—Juvenile fiction.
    [1. Texas—History—Revolution, 1835-1836—Fiction.]  I. Title.

    PZ7.R3647 Me 2001
    [Fic]—dc21                      00-068968
                                      CIP

Republic of Texas Press is an imprint of Wordware Publishing, Inc.
No part of this book may be reproduced in any form or by
any means without permission in writing from
Wordware Publishing, Inc.

Printed in the United States of America

ISBN 1-55622-788-4
10 9 8 7 6 5 4 3 2 1
0101

All inquiries for volume purchases of this book should be addressed to
Wordware Publishing, Inc., at 2320 Los Rios Boulevard, Plano, Texas 75074.
Telephone inquiries may be made by calling:
(972) 423-0090

# 1

Rancho Montoya
outside the town of Gonzales, Texas
September 1835

Only five more days!

Isabel did not think she could wait that long.

Maybe tonight, after everyone else was asleep, she would take the dress from the wardrobe in her room and try it on. Yes, she decided. That is what she would do.

Thinking of how she would look in all that lace made her smile.

"Now there is a pretty sight. What are you smiling about, my Isabelina? Hmmmm?" asked Isabel's father as he tugged on a strand of her long dark hair.

Nicolas Galvez y Montoya was a stocky man with a great, bushy mustache that tickled Isabel's cheeks when he kissed her. She giggled as he did just that.

"Come now *mija*, tell me what puts this lovely smile on your face."

"Oh, I was just thinking, Father," said Isabel.

She did not want to lie, but she could not tell him exactly what she was thinking about. If she did, he might tell her mother.

And Mamma had already told her to leave the dress alone until the wedding.

"Thinking about what?" asked her father. "Could it be you are imagining how you will look in a certain new dress?"

"Oh Father, how did you know?" cried Isabel.

He always seemed to know what she was thinking—almost always.

"It is not so very difficult to figure out my daughter. You have talked of very little else since the dress was finished," he said.

"Father, that is not true! I talk of many things."

"Oh yes," said her father. "You talk of ribbons and bows and pester your mother to let you wear your hair up. You are growing up so fast! Soon it will be your turn to marry."

"Oh no, it will be many years before that happens," said Isabel. "But when I do, I will have a wedding gown even prettier than Feliciana's!"

"I am sure that you will, *mija*," said her father. "Just do not say so to your sister."

He gave his daughter's hair one more gentle tug, then walked off toward the barn. Isabel was alone again on the porch, and that was fine with her. Mother would find her sooner or later, and when she did she would probably have some chore for her to do. Mother never ran out of chores, especially now, with Feliciana's wedding to plan.

Isabel thought about what her father had said. Would she be getting married soon? Her sister was nineteen. She was only eleven. If she got married when she was the same age as Feliciana, it would be eight more years. That seemed a very long time.

I can wait, she thought. Soon Feliciana will have a whole household of her own to care for. And she will probably have children to raise someday soon. No, I do not want such responsibilities now, she thought. All that work! A wedding would be fun though!

Unfortunately, thought Isabel, I cannot have a wedding without getting married!

She decided she would just have to enjoy Feliciana's.

They had been preparing for it for months and months and months, ever since Rodrigo Cantares had asked Father's permission to marry Feliciana.

Rodrigo was an officer in the Mexican army. He was very handsome. Isabel thought he looked dashing in his blue uniform coat, the one with the red cuffs and shiny buttons. He would wear his uniform to the wedding.

Isabel remembered the night Father had announced to the family that Feliciana would marry Rodrigo. Feliciana had cried because she was happy. Mamma had cried, too. She was happy for Feliciana, but sad that she would be going away.

Feliciana would go back to Mexico City with Rodrigo after they were married. Those thoughts made Isabel's smile disappear, just as they had made her mother cry. Mexico City was very far away. She would miss her sister.

It is true that she would still have Alonso and Joaquin and Bartolome, but brothers were not the same as sisters. Besides, Alonso and Joaquin were so serious these days! They were always speaking of the troubles between Mexico and the colonists in Tejas. It seemed nothing else interested them.

And Bartolome was just a baby still in diapers. He was too little to care about politics or weddings.

"What has happened to turn your smile into a frown, *mija*?"

Isabel jumped. She had not noticed her father returning from the barn.

When she told him that she would miss Feliciana, he smiled and hugged her.

"Come with me. I have something that might cheer you up. The cat has given birth to kittens—five of them! Such tiny little things! Their eyes are not yet open. Come see. You can name them."

That was Father, thought Isabel. He did not always understand, but he was always sympathetic.

She leaped off the porch and followed him to the barn.

# 2

**L**ater that night, after dinner and chores, after everyone else had gone to bed, Isabel tiptoed to the wardrobe in the room she shared with her sister. She eased open the door.

"What are you doing, little sister? Didn't Mother tell you to leave the dress alone?"

For the second time that day, Isabel was caught unaware and jumped.

Feliciana, it seemed, was not asleep after all.

"I am just looking at the dress, that is all," said Isabel. And it was true. Even if she had been planning to try on the dress, right now she was only looking at it.

"Yes, I can see that," said Feliciana as she sat up in bed and threw off the covers.

"You know, Isabelina, I think I would like to see you in this dress," said Feliciana. "In fact, I think we should make sure that *your* dress AND *my* dress fit properly. It would not do to put them on the day of the wedding and then find out there is something wrong. What do you think?"

Isabel whipped around to look at her sister.

Feliciana was smiling.

"Oh yes! Let's!" cried Isabel, clapping her hands.

"Sshhhhhhh," said Feliciana. "You will wake up everyone."

She got out of bed. After Isabel had pulled the dress on over her head, Feliciana fastened it up the back. It did not look quite right without petticoats, but it was still very pretty. Isabel was pleased. It was the most grown-up dress she had ever had. The skirt reached almost to the floor!

"You are beautiful, little sister, almost as beautiful as I will be," teased Feliciana. "Come, help me. It is my turn."

For her dress to fit at all, Feliciana first had to put on her corset. She needed Isabel's help with that.

What a silly garment, thought Isabel as she tugged on the strings to cinch in her sister's waist. Wearing corsets was something else she would be happy to wait for. Petticoats were bad enough. All those layers—what did they accomplish except to get in the way and make you hot in the summer?

When they had the corset tied off and Feliciana had donned one petticoat, Isabel helped her sister get into the dress, being very careful not to muss it.

She had to admit; Feliciana was gorgeous. She would be even prettier on her wedding day when she donned the lace mantilla that matched the dress.

Isabel's thoughts from earlier that day flooded over her.

"Oh Feliciana, why do you have to move so far away?" she asked.

"Because that is where Rodrigo will be, you know that Isabelina," said her sister. "But cheer up. I have talked with Mother and Father, and they have given permission for you to come visit when we are settled."

"Really? I can come and stay with you in Mexico City?"

"Yes. Mother and Father have said so."

Isabel had never been to Mexico City. She had never been anywhere except the ranch and Gonzales and San Antonio de Bexar. And as far as she was concerned, that didn't count. Except maybe for San Antonio de Bexar.

Gonzales was just a little village on the banks of the Guadalupe River. When they went there, as they did many times each year, they had to speak English because it was mostly Anglos who lived there. And the Anglos did not speak Spanish.

Isabel had always wondered why people would move to a country and then not learn the language, but her English was not good enough to ask them. Father said the *Americanos* came to live in Tejas for the same reason he had—opportunity.

After the revolution when Mexico freed itself from Spain, the new government offered land to people who would settle the far northern fringes of its territory. She knew Father had accepted the offer because it gave him a chance to be a great *hacendado*, a landowner.

So the family had moved here, to the *frontera*, and she was born on the ranch. Father told her it was a great honor to be the first child born on the new homestead.

Isabel loved the ranch, but sometimes she wished they lived someplace more exciting, someplace like San Antonio de Bexar. She had only been there once, but she had liked it very much.

Her parents had taken her there to celebrate Mexican Independence Day, the anniversary of the time Mexico broke free from Spain. There was a torchlight parade the first night. The church bells rang constantly and someone fired a cannon. Isabel thought she would always remember how the flickering light from the torches played across the walls of the buildings. The next morning, they attended mass. She did not like that part so much. But then they got to go to another parade and listen to speeches and some of the town officials re-enacted the first *grito*, or proclamation, of independence. It was all very exciting. At the end of that day, Feliciana had gotten to attend a fandango, and it was at that dance that she was introduced to Rodrigo Cantares.

Isabel had been too young to go to the dance, but her parents promised her she would be allowed when she was older.

She remembered that San Antonio de Bexar was much bigger than Gonzales and that many *Mexicanos* lived there. They rushed,

rushed, rushed, as if they had important things to do all the time. Yes, she had liked San Antonio de Bexar.

She thought she would like Mexico City even more.

But it would be a very long time before Isabel got to visit her sister there. And when she did finally go, she would still be living at Rancho Montoya but it would be in a different country, the independent Republic of Texas.

Isabel had no way of knowing such things, though.

That night she dreamed of a gleaming city bustling with pleasant people who dressed in beautiful clothes. Best of all, in the dream, gallant *caballeros* in blue coats with red trim threw flowers at her feet and vied for her attention. And she smiled. And was gracious. And she broke all their hearts. And she did it all without wearing a corset.

# 3

The next afternoon, Isabel was in the barn thinking up names for the new kittens when she heard the staccato smack of hooves hitting the ground hard and fast. Someone was riding a horse at a full gallop up the dirt track that led to Rancho Montoya.

Whoever it was must have important news, thought Isabel. Or maybe it was just Alonso and Joaquin racing again. If Father caught them, they would both get in trouble. He had told her brothers repeatedly not to lather up the horses like that.

Isabel cocked her head and listened closely.

No, she decided, no one was racing. There was only one set of hoofbeats. Something important must have happened. The last time such a messenger arrived, he had brought news that her *tio*, her uncle, had died. Tio Carlos lived many days' ride to the west of Rancho Montoya. He had been killed when a band of Comanche raided his farm and set fire to his house.

Isabel shivered remembering that day, and she hoped that no one else had died.

She quickly climbed down from the loft and brushed the stray bits of hay from her clothing. She walked out of the barn just in time to see her brother, Joaquin, thunder up on the gelding he called Sweet Boy.

"Joaquin, what...," but her brother ignored her, much to Isabel's annoyance.

Very much to her annoyance.

He kicked out of the stirrups, leaped to the ground, and sprinted past her to the bell that was mounted on a post in the barnyard. He set it in motion with a mighty yank on its rope and then waited for everyone to gather.

Clang, clang, clang, clang, clang.

It was the signal that drew everyone in case of emergency.

Whatever had happened, it must be very bad.

People came running—from the house, from the fields, from the buildings all over the ranch. Mother arrived clutching Bartolome, and the baby's bottom half was bare. She had been changing him when she heard the bell. Diego, an old ranch hand who had worked for the family as long as Isabel could remember, still had a pitchfork in his hand when he reached them.

Joaquin refused to say a word until everyone had arrived. He just stood there gasping and shaking his head. "No, I want to wait for Father," he said, every time someone demanded that he tell them the news.

When Isabel took her brother a cupful of water from the barrel behind the barn, he smiled his thanks and downed it in one gulp.

Joaquin had caught his breath by the time their father arrived from the far pastures where he had been working that day.

"Who rang the bell? What is happening?"

"It was me, Father," said Joaquin. "I rang the bell. Something awful has happened!"

"Well what is it, boy? Don't just stand there. Tell us what it is!"

"It is what I have been saying would happen," said Joaquin. "The government troops, they are getting out of hand!"

Isabel saw Alonso stiffen.

"What do you mean?" he demanded.

"I have just come from Gonzales," said Joaquin. "Yesterday, a soldier barged into the storeroom in the back of Adam

Zumwalt's shop and beat Jesse McCoy nearly to death! The government no longer has any respect for its citizens!"

"Pah!" scoffed Alonso. "If this is even true, the soldier probably just slapped Jesse to teach him some manners—manners he desperately needs, by the way!"

"Alonso, he beat Jesse with the butt of his musket! He beat him so severely that he lost consciousness," said Joaquin. "No offense could justify that. Besides, those who were there say Jesse did nothing to provoke the man."

Alonso looked somewhat chastened, but he was not ready to back down.

"What happened to Jesse is unfortunate," he said. "But what do they expect when they continue to defy the government? They have no respect for the system they pledged to support."

Joaquin balled his fists and stepped toward his brother. "Alonso, this government *ought* to be defied. Actions like this only prove that to be true."

"Traitor!" cried Alonso, stepping toward his brother.

Isabel held her breath when she saw her father step between his sons.

"*Basta ya!*" he barked. Enough!

"Brother does not fight brother," he said. "Stop this at once!"

For a moment, the only sound was the chirping of a cricket near the barn and the heavy breathing of Joaquin and Alonso. Then both boys stepped back and Isabel released the breath she had been holding. It whooshed from her lungs in a long sigh.

These disagreements between Alonso and Joaquin were getting worse and worse.

Isabel knew they were in big trouble when her mother stepped in.

"My sons, for shame!" she said. And both boys hung their heads.

But their mother was not finished yet.

"We are expecting more than a hundred guests for Feliciana's wedding, and here you are fighting," she said. "It appears you have far more time and energy than you have sense. I can do nothing about the sense, but I have plenty to occupy your time. Come with me."

And off they went—a petite woman with a half-naked baby trailed by two abashed young men.

Isabel pretended to cough and put her hand over her mouth as the comical little group passed so they would not see her laughing. Alonso was twenty-three and Joaquin was twenty-one, but both looked more like schoolboys than grownups at the moment.

They should have known better, she thought, Mother always had something that needed to be done. Politics must make you stupid, she decided.

# 4

Alonso and Joaquin spent the next three days mucking out the outhouses and digging a new one.

Mother must have been very angry to assign them such a task, thought Isabel.

However, she did not have much time to dwell on it. She knew that her brothers would make up. They always did.

She had her own chores to worry about.

The day before the wedding, Isabel found herself outside beating the rugs to get dust out of them. When that was done, she was supposed to wash all the windows, inside and out.

It was hot outside, but she did not mind. After all, she could be stuck inside cooking with the rest of the women, and it was even hotter in the kitchen.

No, she was happy to be out in the fresh air, even if it was fresh hot air.

At that moment, Isabel's mother came out of the house fanning herself.

"Are you not done with the rugs yet, Isabelina?" she asked. "Hurry, child. Hurry. Father Zavala will be here tonight!"

Isabel nodded and started whacking the rugs faster. She had forgotten the priest was arriving a day early.

He certainly has taken his time getting here, she grumbled to herself. I don't see why we have to be so very nice to him. It isn't as if he is doing us a favor. He is only doing his job.

Feliciana had been engaged for more than a year, but she had not been able to get married because there was no one to perform the ceremony. There were only two priests in the whole of the Tejas territory, and they traveled constantly to serve as many people as possible. Wherever they went people cooked for them and gave them gifts.

But Isabel was careful not to say such things within earshot of her mother. She did not want to be assigned to help Alonso and Joaquin!

So she quickly finished the rugs and went to work on the windows. By the time Father Zavala arrived, they sparkled in the late afternoon sunlight.

"Hello, Isabel," called the priest as he dismounted from his horse. "Is it you that I have come to marry?"

Isabel giggled and greeted him. Before she could say anything else, her father emerged from the house.

"Padre, welcome!" he said. "Welcome to our home on this happy occasion."

"*Hola*, Nicolas. I am happy to be here," said the priest. "I wish I brought with me happier news, especially since your Feliciana is marrying a soldier. There is much unrest in the country. I fear things are changing for the worse."

Isabel saw her father look in her direction. Then he said, "Yes, well we have experienced some of that here as well. But let us talk of this another time."

And the two men went into the house, leaving Isabel on the porch until her mother found her and set her to weeding the garden.

Later that night, after her bath, Isabel lay in bed watching Feliciana brush her hair. It would be the last time she and her sister would ever share a room.

Isabel had been looking forward to that, but suddenly the thought made her lonesome. "Feliciana, I am losing you!" she said. "Nothing will ever be the same after tomorrow."

Feliciana turned to look at her little sister, then she put down her brush and walked to the bed. It sagged as she sat on its edge and took Isabel in her arms.

"Isabelina, you will never lose me," she said. "No matter what happens or where I am, we will always be sisters. Nothing can change that."

Isabel would remember this last night before Feliciana's wedding and the words her sister used to comfort her.

# 5

The next day started out as gray and overcast, but nothing could dull the spirits of those who gathered for the wedding. Feliciana was happy, and her family was happy for her.

Isabel donned her new dress and felt as regal as the Queen of Spain.

Father Zavala said mass and married Feliciana and Rodrigo in the front room of the main house at Rancho Montoya. By the time guests began to arrive for the fiesta afterward, the sun had pushed through the clouds.

It was a beautiful day. Isabel thought that was a good omen for her sister.

Isabel flitted around the yard, in and out between the tables loaded with so many good things to eat. Everyone who noticed her complimented her new dress. And she made sure everyone noticed her.

As Isabel skipped past a platter piled high with fresh ears of roasted corn, she saw her father talking with one of their neighbors, Charles Johnson.

Mr. Johnson had not yet complimented her dress. Isabel thought he should have the opportunity to do just that, so she walked to where he was standing with her father.

"I am telling you, Nicolas, this does not bode well for Tejas. Your sons may be hotheaded, but they are not alone. I believe they share the feelings of many people here in the territory," Mr. Johnson said.

"Which one?" asked her father. "They hold opposing views."

"Both," said Mr. Johnson. "That is why it is so dangerous. You have people who want to be loyal to Mexico no matter what, people who want the government to change, and people who want open rebellion and aren't shy about saying so. It's a tragedy waiting to happen."

They were talking about the troubles. Mother would not be pleased if she knew.

Convincing herself that she was doing her mother's will, Isabel interrupted the conversation.

"Hello, Father. Hello, Mr. Johnson," she said. "Mother says we should not talk about the troubles today. She says this is a day for joy, not politics."

"Your mother is a very wise woman," Mr. Johnson replied. "Isabel, may I say that you look lovely today. That dress is quite fetching."

Isabel smiled and thanked him, then dropped a curtsy.

She was pleased with herself. She had gotten Mr. Johnson to notice her dress, and she had enforced Mother's wishes that there be no talk of politics, at least for one day.

# 6

wo weeks after the wedding, Isabel accompanied her father to the general store in Gonzales.

While her father dickered with the shopkeeper over prices, Isabel looked at ribbons and laces. She thought of all the fine dresses she could make with the pretty things.

By the time she heard the commotion outside, she had imagined herself quite an extensive wardrobe. The noises outside put a stop to her daydreams, though. They were too loud for her to ignore.

Mr. Collins and her father must have felt the same way, because they stopped talking and headed for the door of the shop. Isabel started to follow them, but her father held up his hand.

"No, *mija*, you wait here," he said. Then he made eye contact. "I am serious, Isabel. Do not leave this store."

"Yes, Father," she said. He did not often use that tone of voice. He did not often call her Isabel. She had no intention of disobeying him.

Besides, she could see clearly through the store's front window, and she would be able to hear whatever went on if Mr. Collins or her father would leave the store's door open.

With a wink in her direction, Mr. Collins did just that. Then he stepped outside with her father.

Through the window, Isabel could see a mob. There was Mr. Johnson and Mr. Bateman and Mr. Williams. Mr. Arrington was there, too, along with Mr. Dickerson and Mr. Fulcher.

Why, I think every man I've ever met in Gonzales is there, she thought. They seemed to be surrounding something, but she could not see what it was.

The stool!

Isabel remembered that the shopkeeper kept a stool behind the counter. She ran and grabbed it, then dragged it over to the window and climbed up. Instead of sitting on it like Mr. Collins did, she stood on it.

And then she saw.

The men of Gonzales were surrounding...one, two, three, four, five, six—six men, she counted. And each of the six was wearing the uniform of a soldier in the Mexican army.

Isabel was suddenly glad her older brothers had been left at home. This seemed to be a situation that would set them at each other's throats.

"What is going on here?" asked Mr. Collins. "Who are these men?"

"They came to take our cannon," said one of the Gonzales men. Isabel recognized him. It was Albert Martin. He had visited Rancho Montoya. She remembered him as a gentle man. But he did not look gentle now.

No, she decided, he looked angry. Very, very angry.

"What do you mean they came to take it?" asked her father.

"They say they have orders from the military commander in San Antonio de Bexar to take the cannon back with them," said Mr. Martin.

"Is this true?" her father asked one of the soldiers.

Isabel could not hear what the soldier replied, but she could see that he was nodding his head. So it must be true.

Why would the commander want to take the cannon? It was to protect them against Indian attacks.

"Well I don't care what their orders say," said a voice in the crowd. Isabel could not tell whose voice it was. But he kept talking. "We're not going to let them take our cannon, are we boys?"

"No!" came the shout from the crowd.

"No! No! No!"

"What should we do with these fellows?" asked someone else. Isabel thought it was Mr. Dickerson, but she could not be sure.

"Hang 'em!" yelled someone.

"No!" Isabel heard her father say. Then she saw him and Mr. Collins step toward the crowd.

"Drown 'em!" said someone else.

A third person joined in and yelled, "The river! Throw them in the river!"

The crowd seemed to like that suggestion. The men started chanting: "The river! The river! The river! The river!"

Isabel was frightened. She had never seen people behave like this. Were they really going to drown those poor soldiers?

Just then, one of the uniformed Mexicans broke free from the crowd. He darted around a building, with two men from town in pursuit.

The rest of the mob stopped in front of the store with their remaining five captives and waited. In a few minutes the two men from Gonzales returned without the escaped soldier.

"He got away," said one.

Isabel was glad.

"Well come on, then. Let's get the rest of these fellows to the river," said Mr. Martin. And the crowd started chanting again: "The river! The river! The river! The river!"

Isabel saw her father and Mr. Collins step in front of the mob. Oh no! Would they be thrown in the river too, she wondered. Isabel had no idea if her father knew how to swim.

But as it turned out, she had no need to worry. The mob simply ignored them and pushed past with their struggling captives. A few minutes later Isabel heard a great splash followed by raucous laughter.

That was followed quickly by four more splashes and much more laughter.

Isabel was prancing with impatience by the time her father and Mr. Collins returned to the store. They were talking together in low voices and each was shaking his head.

"Father, what happened?" she cried.

"It is alright, Isabelina," he told her. "The soldiers did not drown. They swam across the river after they were thrown in. The only damage, I believe, is to their pride."

He finished his business with Mr. Collins quickly.

"Come, *mija*," he said. "It is time for us to go home."

# 7

Isabel's father rang the bell as soon as they reached the barnyard.

"Why tell them what happened?" she asked. "Won't it just cause trouble?" She was thinking of Joaquin and Alonso.

"They will hear about it eventually," he replied. "It is best that they hear it from me."

"Besides," he said. "This is bigger than your brothers. What happened in Gonzales today could have repercussions for all of us—everyone who lives in or near the town, and that includes Rancho Montoya."

Isabel had not considered that.

When everyone had gathered, he told them what had happened.

Before he had finished speaking, Alonso and Joaquin were eyeing each other.

"Ruffians!" said Alonso, as soon as his father finished speaking. "Tejas is becoming a place where the colonists openly break the law and attack representatives of the government! This must stop!"

As soon as he paused to take a breath, Joaquin weighed in with his opinion.

"Who is breaking the law?" he asked. "What right did the soldiers have to take that cannon?"

"It was the government's cannon," said Alonso. "It was only loaned to Gonzales with the understanding that the town would give it back whenever the army asked. Well, the army asked today and got thrown in the river for its troubles. What does that say about Gonzales?"

Joaquin was ready with an answer, of course.

"It says that we here in Tejas will not be bullied by a craven bunch of *centralistas* in the Mexican government who so fear their own citizens that they would take away our defense against hostile Indians!"

Alonso was incensed. "There is no danger from Indians here," he said. "When was the last time you even *saw* an Indian?"

At that, Joaquin smirked.

"THAT," he said, "is because we have had the cannon for the last four years as a deterrent!"

Alonso was about to reply when his father interrupted.

"Enough of this talk," he said. "I had news and I have shared it. You all still have work to do. Go do it."

"NOW!" he added, when it looked as though Alonso was going to say something else.

"GO!"

And the young men, along with everyone else at Rancho Montoya that day, obeyed him.

But the conversation was far from over.

Joaquin and Alonso continued discussing the situation at supper that night, and the talk soon turned into an argument.

"*Basta ya!*" cried their father, slamming his hand down on the table so hard that the silverware jumped.

"No more! If you two cannot discuss these issues without bickering, then I forbid you to discuss them at all," he said. "You are brothers. Act like brothers."

# 8

After that, everyone seemed edgy and unsettled.

To Isabel, it felt like that hour or so before a summer thunderstorm when she knew that it was coming but it had not yet arrived. She could see the clouds gathering and rushing toward her, then she felt the wind on her face and in her hair. She could even smell it coming. But in that hour before the rain began she was just waiting and waiting.

Right now, they were all waiting, she thought.

I wonder what for?

She found out when, for the third time that month, somebody rang the bell at Rancho Montoya.

It was one of the ranch hands, a young fellow named Mateo Carrera. He had been visiting some relatives in San Antonio de Bexar when he heard the news. And as soon as he heard, he set out for Rancho Montoya. He had come to warn them.

Soldiers—at least one hundred of them—were on their way to Gonzales.

"They will reach the town tomorrow!" Mateo said.

And the town, it seemed, was ready for them. Mateo had had trouble getting across the river at Gonzales because the townspeople had hidden all the boats.

"But the ferry is huge," said Isabel. "How could they hide the ferry?"

"They took it upstream and hid it in the bayou," said Mateo. "And as for the other boats, well they just moved them to the Gonzales side of the river. No one can get across from the San Antonio side, at least not in a boat."

Ah ha! Now Isabel knew he was making up this silly story.

Feeling that she was being very clever she asked, "But Mateo, if there were no boats, how did you get across?"

He grinned at her and said, "I swam."

Of course! Isabel felt foolish.

"You don't mean to say they plan to defy so big a force of soldiers?" asked Alonso.

"Oh yes sir, I believe that is exactly what they mean to do," Mateo replied. "They may not be able to use the cannon themselves, but they will not give it back, either. As I was leaving Gonzales I saw three men wheeling it away. They mean to bury it in a peach orchard to keep it away from the soldiers."

"The fools!" said Alonso at the same moment that Joaquin said, "How brave!"

"Father, we must help them!" said Joaquin.

"No Father, we can't!" cried Alonso. "It would be treason."

Both boys subsided when their father held up his hand for silence.

"Tomorrow, I will go into Gonzales to see what transpires. Then I will decide what we will do," he said. "Until then, I want to hear no more on the subject."

# 9

Isabel got up early the next morning to see her father off.

"Do not be afraid, Isabelina. I will be safe," he said. Then he kissed her and she giggled when his mustache tickled her cheek. She did not feel like laughing, but she did it because her father expected it. That was their routine.

If I pretend everything is normal, she thought, maybe it will be.

She watched her father ride off toward Gonzales, wondering if she would ever see him again. She reached for her mother's hand, and together they watched as long as they could see even the faintest speck of him on the horizon.

*** 

He returned late that afternoon, safe but worried.

"Everything was just as Mateo reported. The cannon and the boats were all hidden," he said.

Everyone who lived and worked at Rancho Montoya had gathered to hear him tell the story of what had happened that day at the river.

"The soldiers arrived in late morning, and they were a splendid sight in their uniforms with the sun gleaming on their buckles and buttons. They looked quite formidable," he said. "But they did not intimidate the men of Gonzales. There were eighteen of them, and they stood on their side of the river, ready to oppose any attempt by the soldiers to cross."

"The Gonzales men did finally allow one courier to swim the river to deliver a message, and that message was that the commander of the troops wanted to speak with the mayor," he continued.

"Now this is where those eighteen men were clever. The mayor is out of town, so they told the soldiers they would simply have to wait for his return. And the soldiers agreed to do so! Can you believe that? They have made camp on DeWitt's Mound across the river, and there they wait. In the meantime, runners have been sent from Gonzales requesting additional men and supplies."

"And what of us, Father?" asked Joaquin.

"What do you mean, my son?"

"I mean, which side do you intend to take? We have plenty of men and supplies to help them right here," Joaquin said.

"Father, no! You cannot mean to help them," said Alonso. "We must help the soldiers. They are doing their duty. They are in the right."

"They are bullies!" cried Joaquin.

And with that, he had gone too far.

Alonso stepped up and punched his brother just below the ribcage. Joaquin struck back with a quick jab that made Alonso's nose bleed.

Isabel rushed to help and got knocked to the ground as her brothers struggled.

"*Basta ya!*" roared her father. "Enough and enough already. Stop it! This is my decision. This fight is between the men from Gonzales and the soldiers from San Antonio de Bexar. We are neither. We are Rancho Montoya. We will not fight for either side."

"But, Father!" both boys cried to his retreating back. But their father did not turn around. He did not even slow down.

# 10

That night Alonso did not come down for dinner.

Isabel was sent to up to his room to fetch him. She knocked, but there was no answer. So she knocked again and waited.

"Alonso?" she said.

No answer.

Finally she opened the door and walked in, thinking that he might have fallen asleep. But no one was there.

Isabel left and returned to the dinner table.

"He is not in his room," she told the family. "Where else could he be?"

When she saw her parents exchange a quick look, Isabel got a sick feeling in her stomach.

At that moment there was a knock on the door. Carlota, the housekeeper, answered it. She returned to the dining room dragging a scared-looking young boy with her. Isabel recognized him. He was the son of one of the ranch hands.

"Go on," said Carlota, cuffing the unfortunate boy on the back of the head. "Tell them. Tell them what you told me."

"Please, sir," he said, reluctantly approaching Nicolas. "I have a message for you from your son. From Alonso. He told me to wait until the evening meal to give it to you.

"Yes, child. Tell me what it is."

"He said to tell you..."

The boy swallowed hard.

"He said to tell you that he has gone to join the Mexican troops and to please not be angry with him."

"No, wait! That is not right," said the lad. "Wait. Wait. He made me memorize his message. He told me to say, 'Father, by now you know that I have gone to fight for my country. I know you must be dismayed. Please try to understand. I feel this is what I must do.'"

By the time the boy finished speaking, Isabel's mother was weeping.

She had wrapped her arms around herself and was rocking back and forth in her chair at the table.

"No, no, no," she said. "Not my boy. Not my boy."

Isabel stared. She had never seen her mother cry.

No one else said a word. What was there to say? Alonso was gone.

After the messenger boy left, everyone stayed at the table but no one ate very much. No one talked. Even Joaquin had nothing to say, and he almost always had a comment on any topic.

That night Isabel lay in her bed, in the room that she now had all to herself, and she thought about her oldest brother.

He was handsome and hard working, and he had always been so very serious. He played the guitar; played like an angel, Mother always said.

And he was kind. Just recently he had helped her bury one of the barn cat's kittens. It was the runt of the litter and was never very strong, but she had cried anyway when it died. Alonso had found her in the barn, cradling its little body in her hands. He interrupted his chores and made a little wooden box for the kitten. Then he helped her bury it behind the barn.

"Do kittens go to heaven?" she had asked.

And he had replied that he did not know. "But I hope so," he said.

Isabel was not really surprised that he had run off and joined the army. He always seemed to think everything was his responsibility. But she wished he had not gone.

She tried to imagine Alonso in the uniform of a soldier: the blue coat with its red cuffs, and the pants with a stripe up the leg; the flat-topped hat with the wide band around its crown; the sword and the gun.

The outfit, which she had always considered so dashing on her brother-in-law, now seemed very ugly to her.

Isabel wondered what Feliciana would think when she found out what Alonso had done. Maybe Rodrigo and Alonso would serve together in the army, but probably not. Rodrigo and Feliciana lived far away.

Alonso had just joined the army at the river.

# 11

Isabel did not sleep much that night. She tossed and turned and dozed fitfully. First she was too warm. Then she was too cool.

Finally she threw back the covers, got out of bed, and put on her clothes. The sun was not yet up.

But I am, thought Isabel.

She decided she would go to the barn and check on the kittens. Their eyes were open now, but she still had not chosen names for them.

It was foggy outside so she made her way to the barn through the swirling white mist. When she got there she was surprised to hear noises coming from inside. Someone else must be awake and worrying about Alonso, too, she thought.

Isabel pulled open the barn door and quietly slipped inside.

Joaquin was there. And he was saddling his horse.

"Joaquin, what are you doing? Why are you leaving so early?" she asked.

Her brother did not stop what he was doing. He did not spare her so much as a glance.

"Good morning, little sister. I am saddling a horse. Surely you can see that," he said.

"Of course I can see that you're saddling a horse," snapped Isabel. "But why are you doing it."

She thought she knew.

"You are going after Alonso, aren't you?" she asked. "You are going to try and stop him from joining the army!"

Joaquin said nothing.

Isabel kept talking.

"I'm sure it is too late," she said. "He must be with them already. And they do not let people unjoin the army, do they?"

"Anything is possible," said Joaquin as he gave the cinch one last tug. Then he turned to his sister.

"Isabelina, I am going, but not after Alonso," he said.

"Then where are you going?" Isabel asked.

"Alonso followed his conscience, and I must follow mine," he replied.

"Joaquin, you are talking in riddles. Speak plainly. Tell me what you intend to do," cried Isabel. She did not like the direction this conversation was taking.

"Very well," he said. "I am leaving but I am not going far. I plan to join the men defending Gonzales."

Isabel was horrified.

First Alonso, now Joaquin.

Then she had a terrible realization.

"Joaquin, if there is a battle you will be fighting Alonso!"

"I know. But I must go," said Joaquin. "Alonso, of all people would understand."

"I will not let you do it!" cried Isabel. "I will not let you. I am going to tell Father!"

She ran, but Joaquin's legs were much longer than hers. He caught her before she reached the barn door.

"Isabelina, listen," he said, crouching down and looking into her eyes. "I am going to join the defenders. It is something I must do and no one can stop me, not even Father. Do not make trouble for me, little one."

He tapped her on the chin with his forefinger. "Promise me. Promise me you will not raise the alarm if I let you go, and I will give you a message to deliver to Father."

Isabel thought about that for a moment, then nodded. She wanted to wake her father, but she knew Joaquin would go whether Father was awake or not. Best to let him go quietly.

She memorized her brother's message to her parents, then she flung herself into his arms and hugged him tightly.

"Promise you will be careful," she said. "Do not do anything foolish, at least not anything too foolish."

He laughed and promised that he would take care of himself, then he led his horse outside. Isabel followed. She wished she had stayed in bed. She did not want to watch him ride away.

Joaquin swung himself into his saddle. Tears pooled in Isabel's eyes.

"Thank you, little sister," he said.

"Some things are so important that they must be done, no matter the personal cost to be paid. This is such a thing for me," said Joaquin. "Someday, you will understand. I promise."

Then he turned, tapped Sweet Boy with his heels, and disappeared into the mist. Isabel could not see to watch her brother go, so she stood there and listened to the fading clip clop of the big gelding's feet hitting the ground as he took her brother away to fight for a cause she did not fully understand.

What was her mother going to say?

# 12

Isabel was not looking forward to telling her parents that Joaquin had gone to join the defenders at Gonzales. So she delayed as long as possible. Her parents would be upset that their sons had defied them and left the ranch. They would be even more unhappy that the boys might end up shooting at each other.

None of this made sense to Isabel. Alonso and Joaquin were always arguing about Mexico and Tejas as if Tejas wasn't a part of Mexico. They talked about the people as if they were two different species, the way they would discuss a cow and a horse.

It was true that the Anglos could be rude sometimes, and they had some odd customs. But they simply did not know any better. And despite what Joaquin said, not all the government officials were corrupt bullies. Some of them, like Rodrigo, were quite charming.

But Alonso always insisted *he* was right, and Joaquin always insisted that *he* was correct and his brother was wrong.

Isabel did not know who to believe. Which side should she choose?

When such thoughts crowded her head, she usually visited the kittens. Playing with them took her mind off the constant arguing between her brothers. So that is where she went next.

All the kittens were fine this morning. Each day they seemed to grow bigger. She picked them up, one by one, and stroked their fur. She nuzzled the last one under her chin. As it began to purr, the tears she had held back finally came.

It seemed like she cried for hours, but when at last Isabel dried her eyes and left the barn, she found that it was still dark outside.

What now? There was nothing to do but wait, so that is what Isabel did.

She sat on the porch and watched the mist swirl around her. This was the time of year, she knew, when the fog would linger. Even late in the morning, there would be little blankets of white in the low-lying places. The Anglos called it will-o'-the-wisp. Isabel thought it was pretty.

She folded her legs beneath her and leaned back against one of the posts that supported the roof of the porch.

Isabel did not move when she heard people moving inside the house.

She was so quiet that her father did not notice her sitting there when he emerged. He walked past her, tromped down the porch steps, and disappeared into the white, misty morning. He saw her when he returned, though.

"Isabelina! Good morning! What are you doing sitting there all by yourself?" he asked.

"I am waiting, Father," she said. It was true, after all.

She followed him into the house and they joined the rest of the household for breakfast—everyone but Joaquin, that is.

He was not there, but only Isabel knew why.

"The boy must still be in bed," said Isabel's father.

He turned to his youngest daughter.

"*Mija*, go fetch your brother," he said.

The time had come. Isabel took a deep breath. Then another.

"It will do no good, Father. Joaquin is not here," she said.

She could have dropped a rattlesnake in the middle of the table and the people around it would not have looked so surprised.

"What do you mean? Has he gone to do chores?" Mother asked.

"No," said Isabel. "He has gone to join the men defending Gonzales. He has given me a message for you."

Then, just like the little messenger boy from the previous night, Isabel recited the words she had been urged to memorize.

"Father," she said. "I have gone to join the brave men of Gonzales. They have asked for help, and I intend to respond to their plea. I truly have no choice. When my brother cast his lot with the *centralistas* in the government, he made the decision for me. I must balance the situation for our family. I must defend our honor. I must fight for a cause I believe in."

The original message had been much longer than that— much, much longer. But Isabel had pleaded with her brother to shorten it, so it would be easier for her to remember. And he did.

Isabel told them the whole story then, about how she had not been able to sleep and had found Joaquin in the barn, about how she pleaded with him to stay home but then finally watched him go. She told them everything.

No one said a word when she had finished.

"Isabel, is this a joke?" Mother asked after a few minutes.

Isabel shook her head. She wished it was.

Her father's shock quickly turned to anger.

"I had ordered him not to leave the ranch," he said. "The boy disobeyed me! He disobeyed! They both disobeyed!"

"I shall disown them both!" he roared.

His wife paid no attention to him. She was too busy scolding Isabel for letting Joaquin leave.

"You should have sounded an alarm. You should have awakened us," Mother said.

Isabel did not think that was fair. She had no control over what Joaquin did.

Her father came to her defense.

"Leave the child alone. She did nothing wrong," he said. "Joaquin should not have put her in such a situation."

Isabel could not have agreed more.

For a time, no one talked. But Isabel had a question she just had to ask.

"Father," she said. "If there is a battle, Alonso and Joaquin will be on opposite sides of it. Will they shoot at each other?"

"Do not talk with your mouth full!" snapped Mother.

"It is a valid question," said Father. "A very good question."

All of a sudden, the cloud of worry that surrounded him seemed to disappear. Isabel could tell he had made a decision.

"My sons will not be put in that position. They will not shoot at each other," he said. "I will not allow that. I am going into Gonzales today, and I will bring them both home."

Isabel was glad.

I would not want to change places with Joaquin or Alonso when Father finds them, she thought. I would not want to be either one of them after he brings them back home, either.

She could not imagine anything worse than having to clean the outhouses, but she was sure her mother would think of something more terrible than that to punish them this time.

And the thought of *that* made Isabel smile for the first time that morning.

# 13

**F**ather left right after breakfast, and Diego went with him.

Diego was more like family than an employee. Isabel even called him Tio Diego, Uncle Diego.

He had worked for the family all his life, ever since he was a young boy. That was back when his hair was a glossy black, not white like it was now. And that was longer than Isabel or any of her siblings had been alive.

Anything that needed doing around Rancho Montoya, Diego could do, and often did. If he did not do it himself, he saw that it got done. Isabel knew that her father trusted him completely.

Diego did not ask if he could go into Gonzales that morning. He did not ask if Isabel's father wanted him for company. He simply saddled his horse and was waiting when the time came.

And then, for the second time that morning, Isabel listened as hoofbeats faded into the misty morning.

I wonder how long it will be until all four of them return? She thought about that as she worked in the kitchen that morning.

She had plenty to occupy her until the men returned. Mother was so glad that Father was going to get Alonso and Joaquin that she was planning a special celebratory meal. That meant much peeling and chopping and mixing for Isabel. But she did not mind. She was glad the boys were coming home.

She was still in the kitchen several hours later when she picked up the sound of a horse—no, two horses—moving fast. Someone was coming to the ranch.

But it was much too soon for Father and Diego to be returning with Alonso and Joaquin. Besides, Isabel could tell from the sound that there were not enough horses—two, not four.

Who could it be?

"Mother, someone is coming," she said.

They both wiped their hands then went to the front porch to see who it was. The fog had burned off by that time, and they could see a lone rider coming up the path toward the house leading another horse.

He was bringing them something; Isabel could see it strapped to the second horse, a great dark blob across the saddle.

That looks an awful lot like Father's horse, thought Isabel.

Then she realized it *was* her father's horse. At the same moment, she realized that the "something" draped across the horse's saddle was her father.

She rushed down the steps beside her mother when the horses stopped. Together with Diego, they got Nicolas Galvez y Montoya off his horse and carried him into the house. They put him in his bed.

Only then did her mother ask what had happened, though by that time it was obvious, even to Isabel.

"Oh, señora," said Diego, shaking his head. "Nicolas has been shot."

Diego's Story:

We left, just the two of us this morning, moving toward Gonzales as fast as we could in the fog. We decided early on that we would stop in the town first, as our chances of finding Joaquin quickly were much greater than our chances of finding Alonso.

We presumed Alonso would be on the other side of the river someplace with the government troops.

Nicolas intended to send Joaquin home, after a good scolding of course. Then we would find a way to cross the river and look for Alonso.

We were determined that both boys would be home tonight, sleeping in their own beds as they ought to be. Yes, that was the plan and it was a good one.

We were discussing this plan as we neared the town. It never occurred to us to be on our guard. This is our home; what did we have to fear?

A great deal, as it turned out. We should have been more careful.

For suddenly, we heard a voice say: "Halt. Halt. Do not come any closer. Identify yourselves—friend or foe?"

We were startled, as you might imagine. And we stopped.

"Friend!" cried Nicolas as we sat there on our horses in the fog.

Several men on foot appeared, some in front, some on the sides, some behind. Eight or nine in all. They were Anglos, but we did not recognize any of them. They were not men from Gonzales.

I thought they were highwaymen. I thought they were going rob us. But they took nothing from us. They only looked at us.

"Who are you?" barked one of the men, the one who seemed to be the leader of the little gang. He was holding on to the bridle of Nicolas' horse. Normally of course, we would not stand for such treatment. But these are tense times, and they tend to make men edgy. Besides, we were outnumbered.

So Nicolas identified us.

"I am Nicolas Galvez y Montoya from the Rancho Montoya near here, and this is my friend Diego Munoz. He is also from Rancho Montoya," he said.

Then he said, "What is the meaning of this? Let us pass!"

"Simmer down," said one of the other men. "We decide who gets to pass and who don't, and we ain't decided about you yet."

Another of the men said, "We can't let them go. They're Mexicans. Look at them. We can't have them informing to the enemy about us."

"I think they probably *are* the enemy," said a third man.

Nicolas was losing his patience.

"Preposterous," he huffed. "I am going into Gonzales to look for my son. I demand that you let us pass."

"I'm sorry, sir, but I can't let you do that," said the leader.

"I am not asking you. I am telling you!" cried Nicolas. Then he kicked at the leader and urged his horse forward.

I followed, of course. That is when I heard the shots. They seemed to come from all directions at once. And Nicolas slumped over in his saddle.

When I caught his horse, Nicolas was still conscious.

"Find Joaquin and Alonso," he said. "Do this for me, old friend."

I could see that he was in bad shape, and so I decided to take him on in to Gonzales in hopes of finding a doctor.

But the men—more of them this time—surrounded us again.

"Looks like we got us some Mexican spies," said one of them.

I repeated what your father had said, but it did not seem to make a difference. The ruffians were determined to see us as the enemy.

"Get one of the men from Gonzales here to identify us," I pleaded. "Please, my friend is hurt."

"Well you should have thought about that before deciding to spy on us!" said another of the men.

At that point, I lost my temper, too.

"We are not spies!" I yelled. "I do not even know who you are."

That is when they pulled us off our horses and tied our hands behind our backs. They tied Nicolas' hands even though he was unconscious. They did finally bandage his wound, but only after I pleaded relentlessly.

Finally, they sent someone into Gonzales to get Adam Collins, from the store. They did not believe we were innocent, but they wanted to make absolutely sure we were spies before they hanged us.

(At this point in Diego's story, Isabel heard her mother gasp.)

After what seemed a very long time, Mr. Collins and another man from town, Albert Moore, returned with the strangers.

They immediately identified us and demanded that we be released. We were untied, and we did what we could for Nicolas before hoisting him onto his horse and tying him on tight.

Then I got on my horse and brought him home. And here we are.

*** 

Isabel was furious.

"Who are these men who shot my father?" she demanded.

"They are volunteers, Isabelina," said Diego. "When the troubles about the cannon started, a call for help went out and men have been flooding into Gonzales from other towns ever since. I am told their numbers now equal the numbers of the soldiers sent by the government."

Isabel decided she had been right all along. Politics did make people stupid.

Her father had been wounded very badly. Two bullets had struck him, and both went completely through his body—one through his right shoulder, the other through his side. There was a lot of blood, more blood than Isabel had ever seen before from a human being.

After Diego told them his story, he said he would try to complete the failed mission. He wanted to go find Joaquin and Alonso.

Isabel was surprised when her mother told him not to go.

"We need you here, Diego," she said. "My sons are grown men, and they will have to live with their choices."

# 14

Nicolas had not regained consciousness by that evening, and Isabel was worried about him. The bleeding had stopped, but her father seemed to be running a fever.

She sat by his side and bathed his face with a rag dipped in cool water. She had a cup ready in case he woke up and was thirsty. But so far his eyes had remained closed.

Isabel knew her mother must be worried, but it was impossible to tell from looking at her. She went about her daily chores, and she talked with Diego about what needed to be done on the ranch.

She was very calm, very collected. She had not cried once.

"No! No!"

Isabel was startled by her father's outburst.

"What is it, Father?" She leaned over and looked into his face, but his eyes were still closed. There was sweat beaded along his hairline and across his nose.

"No!" he said again.

She decided he must be dreaming.

"Sshhh, Father. I am here," she said while blotting his forehead with the rag.

Her father tossed his head and thrashed in the bed. Isabel was afraid he would make his wounds start bleeding again if he did not settle down.

"Mother! Mother, come in here," she called, raising her voice so it would carry into the next room. "Father needs you."

Her mother was there before she finished the sentence. She bent over her husband, put her hand on his forehead to gauge his temperature, then checked his bandaged wounds. As Isabel had feared, they had begun to bleed.

Isabel's father muttered during his wife's quick examination, occasionally bursting out with a "No!" or another word or phrase that Isabel could sometimes understand. But he did not seem aware of his surroundings. He did not know that they were there.

There was a question Isabel had wanted to ask her mother ever since Tio Diego brought her father back to Rancho Montoya. Until now, she had not known how to ask or had simply not had the nerve *to* ask.

"Mother, is he going to die?" said Isabel.

It had taken her all day to work up enough courage to broach the subject. Now that she had, she was not sure she wanted to hear the answer.

"I do not know, *mija*. Truly, I do not know. I wish that I did," her mother replied.

Father was muttering again.

Isabel could pick out the words "careful" and "sons" and "no." She asked her mother what it meant.

"He is worried about your brothers, I think," her mother replied. "It is hard to tell exactly."

Bartolome began to cry in the other room. He needed to be fed or changed or both. So Isabel was left alone again with her father, while her mother went to tend to the baby.

Isabel did not know much about such things, but it seemed to her that her father was growing weaker.

"Do not feel responsible," her mother said later. "We are doing everything we can, and you are a great help to me. I am sure you are a comfort to your father. He lost a lot of blood.

When that happens, time is the only cure, and it does not always work."

Throughout that night, Isabel slept on a pallet beside her father's bed. He tossed and talked under his breath to himself on and off.

From listening to him for such a long time, Isabel thought she had figured out what he was saying. It was as Mother had said; he was worried about Alonso and Joaquin.

But he was also angry with them for leaving Rancho Montoya in the first place. And he felt responsible that they had.

Isabel was sure he felt responsible, though she could not understand why he would feel that way.

She wondered what Alonso and Joaquin would say if they knew their father had been wounded.

And at that moment, an idea took root in her mind. It flowered throughout the night and was in full bloom by the time the sun came up the next morning.

# 15

When she woke up, her father seemed worse, so her mother decided to send for a doctor. Because of what Diego had said about what was happening in Gonzales, Isabel's mother sent a ranch hand to the nearby town of Columbus to find a healer.

It would take him most of that day to get to the town and return with a doctor. And that was if a doctor was available and could travel right away.

As she had the previous day, Isabel stayed by her father's side. She daubed at his forehead with the rag, held his hand, and periodically checked his wounds.

Sometime in the midmorning she dozed off, so she thought she was dreaming when she heard her father moan and say, "It is my fault, you know."

Isabel snapped awake and looked at her father. His eyes were open.

"Welcome back to us, Father," said Isabel in the soft voice her mother insisted she use in the sickroom.

He father moaned. "What happened to me?" he asked, and then he grimaced as he tried to sit up.

"What happened?!" he asked again, this time more insistently.

He was obviously in pain, but he knew what he was saying.

"You went to find Alonso and Joaquin, Father, and you were shot accidentally," she told him. Then she called to her mother, who came running.

"Who?" he asked.

"It is me, Nicolas. Your wife," said Isabel's mother.

"No, no," he said. "Who shot me?"

So Isabel told him the story Diego had told her and her Mother. By the time she had finished the tale, her father was looking very weak. But he was still conscious.

He grasped both of her mother's hands in one of his own as he struggled to force words out of his frail body.

"It is my fault they left," he said. "Alonso and Joaquin—I was too harsh with them. I should have listened. I should have tried to understand. I have forgotten what it was like to be a young man."

Isabel backed out of the room as her mother tried to comfort him.

"Nicolas, you are a good father..." she was saying as Isabel slipped away.

***

She had been right! Father did feel responsible.

And now he was dying, of that she was absolutely certain.

He was dying, and her brothers did not know. He was dying, and it was all their fault. If they had not run away, he would not have had to go after them. He would not have gotten shot.

Well, she was going to find them and tell them. That was the plan she had been working out all night as her father mumbled to himself.

She would find her brothers and make them come home.

Isabel decided to leave right after lunch.

She did not tell her mother or Diego or anyone else. If they knew, they would only forbid her from going and then she would have to disobey. This way, she was not being naughty because she had not been told not to do what she was *determined* to do.

Now she had to find a way to get off the ranch without her mother becoming suspicious.

She had worked out several possible scenarios and was trying to decide which one to use when her mother supplied the perfect excuse.

"Isabelina, you are spending too much time in the sick-room," Mother said over lunch. "You have been with your father constantly since Diego brought him back from Gonzales. After we eat, I want to you go outside. Get some fresh air, play with the kittens. Why not go for a ride? How long has it been since you took Beauty out?

Of course! Beauty! Beauty was her pony. Isabel realized her mother had just supplied her with a means of escape.

But she knew she should not agree too quickly to her mother's suggestion. If she did, her mother would be suspicious. So Isabel argued instead.

"But what if Father gets worse? I want to be there," she said.

"If he gets worse, I will ring the bell," said Mother. "You will be able to hear that no matter where you are on the ranch."

"Mother, are you sure?" asked Isabel.

"Yes, you need to get out. Your father will be fine."

Isabel knew that was not true. She knew her father was very, very sick. But she finally agreed to go. She had a mission to complete.

First, she changed into her riding clothes, an old pair of Joaquin's castoff trousers and a shirt. Isabel rode like a boy. She straddled the horse. Mother said that she would have to learn to ride sidesaddle, like Feliciana, when she grew up. Isabel thought that was a silly way to ride and did not want to learn.

After changing her outfit, she saddled Beauty. It always took at least an hour because Beauty liked to play. Isabel always had to check the cinch at least three times before she could ride. Beauty puffed up like a fiesta cake when she saw the saddle coming. Isabel had to put the saddle on and cinch it, wait awhile, and cinch it down again. Then she had to repeat the whole process at least once more. Otherwise the saddle would slip right off the tubby little horse. Beauty also liked to toss her head around to avoid the bridle.

It was midafternoon by the time Isabel was ready to go.

She was fairly certain she could be back before dark. It would all depend on how long it took her to find her brothers.

# 16

"Halt! Who's there?"

The challenge came from somewhere to her right.

She decided to ignore it. She had no time for trigger-happy Anglos.

"Stop! Stop or I'll shoot!" said the voice.

Her father had stopped and they shot him anyway. She dug her heels into Beauty's flanks and laid low over the pony's neck as it leaped into a gallop.

"Stop! Stop!" came the cries from behind her.

Isabel heard the crack of a rifle. Then she heard horses pounding after her. She urged Beauty on. "Go, girl, go," she whispered.

Beauty tried, but she was a pony, and her little pony legs were no match for the long-legged horses chasing her.

Less than five minutes later, in spite of Beauty's best effort, Isabel's pursuers caught up with her.

Isabel slowed her pace. There was no sense in exhausting the little animal. Six men on horseback surrounded her.

"It's a girl!" she heard one of them say.

"Let me go!" she demanded. "I have done nothing to you. You have no right to stop me!"

Would they shoot her like they had shot her father?

"She could be a spy," said another man.

"She's just a child. Look at her," said a different voice. "She's no spy. She's scared to death. A spy wouldn't look so scared."

Isabel *was* frightened, but it made her angry that these men could tell.

She assumed her haughtiest look, the one she had learned by watching Mother deal with pertinent shop clerks. "You have already shot one Montoya this week," she said. "Isn't that enough?"

None of the men seemed to know what she was talking about.

"Montoya. Isn't that the name of the new volunteer?" said the man who was now holding Beauty's bridle. He called over his shoulder, "Hey, Jack, you know that new kid, the one who came in yesterday; did he get shot?"

"No, why?" replied the man who must be Jack.

Montoya! A new volunteer named Montoya! They must be talking about Joaquin!

Suddenly, Isabel felt happy to see these men.

"Please," she said. "You must take me to see this new volunteer. He is my brother. I must see him!"

She looked around her. All six men were staring.

So she repeated herself, speaking slowly this time so they would understand.

"Well, we can't leave her out here no matter who she is," said the one they called Jack. "I guess we ought to take her along with us. We can let the colonel figure out what to do with her."

\*\*\*

Twenty minutes later, Isabel found herself standing in front of a beefy, red-faced man. The one called "colonel" by the others was not in the camp. This man was in charge while he was gone. The other men called him Jackson. Isabel wondered if that was his first name or his last name.

Isabel thought he was the dumbest person she had ever met.

She wanted to see Joaquin and kept saying so, but Jackson did not seem inclined to grant her request.

"Not so fast," said the man. "Who did you say you are?"

Isabel sighed. He had asked her that question twice already.

But she told him her name—again. And she told him where she was from—again. And she told him about her father getting shot. And she asked to see her brother—again.

And Jackson ignored her request—again. Instead, the man stood up and loomed over her. He was a big man and Isabel was a small girl, so the light from the setting sun threw his shadow over Isabel like a blanket. Suddenly, she felt like a small animal being eyed by a buzzard.

"You must be angry about your Pa getting hurt," he said. "That seems like a pretty good reason to be a spy for the other side. You and your brother could be in it together."

Isabel stared. Was the man loco?

"Joaquin doesn't even know that Father is hurt," she said. "I told you that already. Now please, please let me talk with him! Our father is dying and my brother doesn't know."

"No girl, you don't fool me," the man called Jackson finally said. "I think you're a spy for the Mexican army. You ain't goin' nowhere."

He stepped toward her, and before Isabel knew what was happening he had tied her wrists behind her back, and he tied them tightly. Her fingers began to tingle as they lost circulation.

Isabel had had enough of this man and his craziness. She opened her mouth to scream, but Jackson was waiting for her to do that. He slipped a gag into her mouth. Then he knelt and tied her ankles together and pushed her to the ground under the tree that had sheltered their little talk.

"That'll keep you quiet, spy girl," said her captor. He chuckled as he walked off to join the other men.

Isabel could not believe what was happening. She was trussed up like a bird about to be cooked for dinner. She had not seen Joaquin. These stupid men thought she was a spy. And the sun was going down.

From where she lay under the spreading branches of an enormous oak tree, Isabel could see the shadows getting longer and the light getting less intense. She would not be getting home by dark after all.

Soon, Mother would realize that she and Beauty were missing.

# 17

Isabel finally got to see Joaquin, but she couldn't talk with him.

He landed with a grunt next to her on the ground underneath the tree by the river. Like her, his hands and feet were tied. Like her, he had been gagged.

"Joaquin!" she cried. But it came out sounding more like "Wawing!" thanks to the scrap of cloth that was stuffed in her mouth.

His attempts to talk back met with similar, garbled results.

Joaquin rolled onto his stomach, pulled his knees underneath his body, and managed to sit up.

Isabel did the same

Joaquin knee-walked to where she was, then turned his back on her.

Isabel was puzzled until she felt him plucking at the cord that bound her hands. He was trying to free her!

As her brother's fingers wrestled with the knot at her wrists, Isabel imagined their escape. They would sneak to where the horses were tied, get Beauty and Sweet Boy, and ride into the night! No, they had to find Alonso...

"Ouch!" yelped Isabel, clearly enough to be understood through the gag. Joaquin mumbled something that could only have been an apology. In his attempt to untie her, he had twisted the rope and it bit hard into her skin. She'd have a mark there for sure. But her brother was trying to help. She mumbled back an acceptance of his apology.

Then she went back to her imaginings. They would need to find Alonso, and he was probably on the other side of the river. So they'd have to get a boat. But Mateo had said the townspeople hid all the boats. Well, maybe they could steal—no, not steal, *borrow* one. That's it. They'd *borrow* a boat to cross the Guadalupe, one big enough so they could ride the horses right up into it and across they'd go.

Isabel imagined waving gaily to the stupid rebels who would be standing on the bank, trying to figure out how Isabel and Joaquin had gotten away.

She flexed her wrists and could feel that the rope binding them was looser. Joaquin was going to set her free. It took him another two or three minutes, but then Isabel felt the rough cord slide off. She was free! Well, her hands were, at any rate.

She reached up to remove her gag.

"See! They're trying to escape!"

Isabel looked over her shoulder and saw the big stupid man named Jackson running toward her. Another man, one Isabel had not see before, followed him at a slower pace.

"Told you they was spies," said Jackson as he grabbed Isabel and jerked her roughly to her feet.

Joaquin threw himself at Jackson, but the man sidestepped and Joaquin landed on the ground again. Isabel started wriggling. If she could just get one hand up near Jackson's face, she felt certain she could scratch him hard enough to make him let go. From the corner of her eye, she saw Joaquin start rolling in their direction. Tied up or not, they were going to fight!

"Let the girl go! Untie them you fool!" barked the stranger with Jackson.

All three of them—Jackson and Isabel and Joaquin—turned to stare at the man.

"You heard me! Untie them! Do it NOW!" he said.

"But Colonel, they're *spies!*" said Jackson.

"Of course they're not. Untie them. Don't make me tell you again," said the stranger.

Isabel was beginning to like the fellow.

Jackson dropped her wrists and reached to untie her gag, but she knocked his hand away and took off the gag herself. Then she turned her back to him, sat down, and started working on the knot at her ankles.

She wanted to say something to Jackson—something elegant and haughty and vicious. But she was using all her strength not to cry at the moment so she simply ignored the brute. Relief warred with anger inside her as she finished untying herself.

"Señorita, my apologies," said the stranger. "I am sorry this has happened. It has been a terrible misunderstanding."

"It certainly has!" said Isabel.

"You'll regret this, Colonel. I'm tellin' you, they're spying for the government troops," said Jackson as he finished untying Joaquin. "If they weren't, why'd they try to get away?"

"Jackson, *anybody* would try to escape if you tied them up," said the newcomer. "Father Zavala, Pastor Clark...I dare say your own mother would try to get away if you tied her up."

"My mother died when I was just a boy, sir," said Jackson.

"Never mind. Just go join the other volunteers," said the man. Then he turned his attention to the recently freed brother and sister.

"Joaquin, I'm sorry about this," he said.

"Well sir, at least the men are doing their jobs," said Joaquin. Then he shook hands with the stranger.

Isabel could not believe her eyes. Joaquin must be getting as stupid as Jackson. Maybe it was catching.

"Sir, this is my little sister, Isabel," said Joaquin. "Isabel, this is Col. John Henry Moore. He's our leader."

"Hello, Isabel," said Col. Moore. "Welcome to the resistance."

But Isabel ignored him and turned to her brother.

"What do you mean 'our' leader?" she demanded. "You can't intend to stay here and fight with these stupid men who tied you up!"

"Isabel, for shame!" said Joaquin.

"I'm sorry, sir," he said over Isabel's head to Col. Moore. "She's a little upset right now."

"I can certainly understand that," said the colonel. "You do intend to stay with us, don't you Joaquin? We need every good man we can get."

"Yes sir, I'm with you," Joaquin said. Then he turned to his sister.

"Isabel, what are you doing here?" he asked.

She had been so frightened and angry about being tied up, that she had forgotten her original reason for leaving Rancho Montoya.

"I came to fetch you and Alonso. You must come home," she said. "Father is dying. He is dying and he says it is his fault that you and Alonso ran away. He says it is his fault that you are now on opposite sides of this battle."

"That is a terrible lie to tell, just because you don't want me to fight with these men," Joaquin said.

He didn't believe her. He didn't *want* to believe her.

"I am telling the truth," she said. "Ask your so-called 'friends' here. Before they started attacking eleven-year-old girls, they shot Father. Twice. Diego saw it happen. "

Joaquin turned to Col. Moore.

"Is this true?" he asked.

"A man was shot by accident two days ago," replied the colonel. "I did not know he was your father, and I did not realize his

wounds were so severe. I'm sorry, Joaquin. This makes everything different. I realize that you must leave us."

Joaquin turned and leaned on the tree.

The colonel turned to Isabel.

"Ma'am, I really am sorry about what's happened," he said.
"Can I get you anything? Would you like some water?"

The man was being so exceedingly polite that Isabel did not
have the heart to continue being rude. Besides, she was very
thirsty.

So she gave the colonel a slight smile and told him she would
appreciate some water. "But don't let that Jackson person bring it
to me!" she called as he walked away to fulfill her request.

Isabel turned toward her brother. But when he realized that
she was walking in his direction, he waved her off.

"Give me some time to think," he said.

So Isabel turned away and walked a few steps in the other
direction. She watched the river. It was dark now, but the water
caught glints of light and reflected them.

She heard something upstream, but before she could identify
it, Col. Moore returned with a tin cup full of water for her.

Isabel thanked him and drank it quickly.

Joaquin joined them.

"Sir, are the plans for tonight the same?" he asked the
colonel.

"Yes," said Col. Moore.

"What plans?" asked Isabel.

"We're going to sneak across the river and attack tonight,"
Joaquin told her. Then he turned back to the colonel.

"Count me in, sir," said Joaquin.

"What?" Isabel exclaimed. "Joaquin, didn't you hear me?
Father is *dying*."

"I heard you," said her brother. "But there is nothing I can do for him. I can do something here—something good. That is my decision."

Isabel knew her brother well enough to recognize that tone of voice. He was staying.

But she was going.

Maybe Alonso wouldn't be so pig-headed.

# 18

Isabel hugged her brother good-bye.

Then she tried to step away, but Joaquin kept his grip on her arm.

How sweet, thought Isabel. He hates to see me go. He must love me very much.

"Col. Moore, I think you should bring some of that rope over here," said Joaquin.

Isabel wondered what her brother was talking about.

Col. Moore apparently wondered the same thing because he asked Joaquin what he was up to.

"Sir, I know my sister," he said. "She came out here to find me and my brother, and my brother is serving with the government troops. As soon as she leaves here she'll head across the river. And she knows our plans, sir. I think we need to keep her here until after the attack, for everyone's safety."

"What?!" shrieked Isabel. "Joaquin, you're not serious! You can't keep me here!"

She wrenched her arm away from him and started running, but it was a simple matter of a few strides for him to catch up with her.

"Men's lives are at stake, Isabel. I know you mean well, but I must do what I think is best," Joaquin said as Isabel struggled in his grip.

Isabel appealed to Col. Moore. He had been so pleasant and reasonable, and she hadn't been too terribly rude to him.

"Stop him, sir. You can't let him do this," she said.

Col. Moore turned to Joaquin. "If you explain the situation, wouldn't she stay here on her own?" he asked.

"Ask her for yourself, sir."

So Col. Moore did.

Isabel's glare was enough to answer his question for him. He shook his head.

"I hate to do this, but I'm afraid your brother is right," he said.

Isabel was stunned. The stupidity was spreading. It seemed all the men here were infected. She wondered if it had crept across the river and infected the Mexican troops, too. If it had, they were all in trouble.

Col. Moore gave Joaquin a length of rope, then he pulled a handkerchief from his back pocket.

"Here," he said. "Fold this and put it under the rope. It should make things a bit more comfortable for you sister. And tie her hands in front of her, not in back."

"I don't think that is a good idea, sir," said Joaquin.

"We have to detain her, but we don't have to treat her like criminal," said Col. Moore. "Tie her hands in front, then tie her to the tree."

Joaquin did as he was told.

"Isabel, please just accept this. It is for your good as much as for ours," he said.

"Joaquin, when you untie me I will punch you in the nose, and I hope you understand because *that* will be for *your* own good," she said.

When Joaquin finished binding her hands, he pushed Isabel so her back was against the tree trunk. Then he looped a longer piece of rope around her midsection in order to tie her to the tree.

This must be how Beauty feels about being saddled, thought Isabel.

Then she smiled. Thinking of the pony had given her an idea.

She took a deep breath, sucking as much air into her lungs as possible, then she arched her back away from the tree just slightly.

That should do it, she thought, as Joaquin tied the knot.

One of the volunteers approached as her brother was finishing the job.

"The ferry is almost here, Col. Moore," said the man, looking curiously in Isabel's direction.

"Thank you, Williams, we'll be right there," replied the colonel. Then he turned to Joaquin.

"Finish up here, son, then join us at the ferry. And be quick. If we're going to take the government troopers by surprise at dawn, we need to get started," the colonel said.

He said goodbye to Isabel, but she ignored him, so he left.

Joaquin double-checked the knots holding Isabel. He patted her arm and said goodbye. She ignored him, too, so he turned and started walking away.

But Isabel couldn't let him leave like that. Angry as she was with him, he was still her brother and she loved him.

"Joaquin?" she called. He looked over his shoulder.

"Good luck," she said. "Be careful."

# 19

Isabel sat, bound and fuming, as the eager volunteers piled onto the ferry with their horses and their gear.

That must have been the sound she had heard earlier coming from upstream, she thought. The men had retrieved the ferry from its hiding place so they could use it.

They made so much noise—talking and laughing, clinking and clanging—that Isabel did not see how the government troops would be at all surprised. Surely the rebellious settlers could be heard all the way to Mexico City, she thought.

Well, Isabel decided, she wasn't going to just sit there and do nothing. When she was certain Joaquin was not coming back, she started wiggling. The deep breath she'd taken when her brother tied her had given her just enough room to maneuver.

Slowly, slowly, she worked the rope up toward her shoulders.

She twisted and squirmed and shrugged until, finally, the rope moved past her shoulders. She ducked her head under the loop, and she was free—almost. Her wrists were still tied.

Isabel had already thought about how to handle that. She started walking toward the river, all the while scanning the ground for sharp rocks.

When she found one, Isabel picked it up then sat down and held it between her knees while she sawed her wrists back and forth against the sharp edge.

It was working! The rope was fraying!

It was taking a long time, though. She had to stop once, when the rope had been cut halfway through, to rest her arms.

Isabel had no idea how long she had been sitting there, raking her bonds against the stone, when the cord finally frayed enough to break. It slipped off her wrists.

She wanted to shout with triumph, but she dared not do it. She did not want to be captured again.

Instead, she made her way to the river, hoping to find a boat. She knew that she had to get across somehow. But there was no boat. She walked and walked along the river's edge, but she could not find one.

Mateo must have been right. The townspeople had hidden all the boats.

Now what? She had to get across the river, and she did not want to swim. Isabel remembered that Mateo had said the river was running swift and strong because of the recent rains.

She sat down on a fallen log to think about it. But she could come up with no better solution.

I guess I'll just have to swim, she decided.

Isabel stood up. And as she did, her eyes fell on the log.

Of course! If the log would float, she could ride it across. It was already right at the water's edge. It should not take much effort to get it into the water.

Isabel walked all the way around the fallen tree. It was about six feet long and its inside layers were rotting away. That was good because it would make it lighter and easier to handle. The log was big enough for her to sit on, too.

Next, she eyed the river. She could not see the far bank. Fog was creeping in.

That could be good, too, she decided. Yes it would prevent her from seeing where she was going. But it would also keep her from being *seen*. And considering the events of this day so far, that was a very good thing as far as she was concerned.

All right Isabel, quit stalling, she told herself. Just get it over with. This won't be as bad as being tied to a tree—by your *brother*, of all people.

If Joaquin thought she would let this pass quietly, he was quite mistaken. She had every intention of coming up with a suitable act of revenge.

She was stalling again.

Time to get across that river.

First, Isabel took off her riding boots and hid them under a bush along the riverbank. She did not want to ruin them in the river. She took the ribbon that had been holding her hair and tied it to the bush so she could find it, and her boots, later.

Then she tried to shift the tree. It moved easily. Back and forth, back and forth... she rocked the tree until it suddenly broke free of the sandy soil and rolled right into the river with a soft plop.

Isabel ran into the shallows after it.

The muddy river bottom squished up between her toes as she slowly guided the tree into the Guadalupe. When she was standing knee-deep in the river, Isabel threw her right leg over the log just like she would mount a horse. (No sidesaddle for her!) Then she pushed off, and the old tree slowly floated into the current.

# 20

It took Isabel about thirty seconds to realize she had made a very bad decision.

The log rolled almost immediately and dumped her into the water. She bobbed right up, but the world was dark. Her long hair was plastered over her face, and she could not see anything.

She clawed her hair away from her eyes just in time to see the end of the log whipping past her. The current was stronger than she had thought—definitely too strong for her to swim all the way across.

Two quick kicks reunited her with the tree, but she could not pull herself back up on top of it. Every time she tried, it just rolled. So she could not get on the tree and she could not get across the river without it.

She would just have to stay in the water and hang on to the tree until she was close enough to the other riverbank to swim for it.

Not that she could see the other bank. In fact, she could not see land on either side of the river. The fog had rolled in thick and heavy.

Maybe I can't swim across, she thought, but I *can* kick.

So she kicked. And she was pleased to feel the log move in the direction she thought she wanted to go. So she kicked some more.

Isabel had no idea how long she had been in the river when she finally felt the log scrape into the shallows once more. She tried to stand up, but her legs quivered and refused to hold her and she splashed into the Guadalupe.

It was shallow where she fell, so Isabel slowly pulled herself onto her hands and knees. And inch by inch, she crawled out of the river.

# 21

At first she just lay there catching her breath and appreciating the feel of the land beneath her.

But Isabel could not forget why she had braved the river in the first place. She had to find Alonso. Maybe together they could find Joaquin again and this time convince him to return home with them.

Father could be dead already for all that she knew. But she had to try.

The problem now was that she was not sure which way to go. Where was Alonso?

Back in the other camp she had heard one of the men say that the Mexican troops had moved upstream. Well, the current had most certainly just taken her downstream, she reasoned.

So I'll walk along the river in the opposite direction of the current, she decided.

She took one step and realized that she would have to make the entire journey barefooted. Her boots were still on the other side of the river.

Oh no! What next?

She had only two choices: stay here or move on. Summoning an image of her father lying wounded in bed, she chose the second option.

\*\*\*

The fog not only made it hard to see where she was going, it distorted sounds, too.

Isabel thought she heard horses and riders several times, but she could not tell where the sound was coming from. She couldn't see enough, and she was hearing *too* much.

Owls hooted nearby, and creatures she could not see scrabbled in the undergrowth. Isabel estimated that she had been walking for at least three hours.

At first, she kept her head down so she could watch where she stepped. But several low branches had taken her by surprise and whipped across her face. Now her face was scratched and bleeding, her feet were scratched and bleeding, and she was as tired as she could ever remember being.

She had to keep reminding herself why she was out here.

Finally, she just had to rest.

I can't take another step unless I sit down for just a few minutes, she thought.

In this area, there were many big, flat-topped rocks protruding from the ground. Isabel sank onto the next one she came across. She examined her sore feet and found that one toenail had been ripped away completely.

When did that happen? She wondered.

As she examined the damage, Isabel became aware of a new sound. It was something moving through the underbrush, but it sounded a lot bigger than a raccoon or opossum.

Well, if I can't see it then it can't see me so there is no cause to be afraid, she reasoned.

Still, going just by the events of the last few days, Isabel thought she should be careful.

She slipped off the rock and crouched behind it.

"Where are we? I can't see a thing out here!"

Isabel jumped. The voice sounded like its owner was standing behind her. *Right* behind her. She didn't dare move. She didn't dare to make a sound. She pressed her cheek against the smooth cool surface of the rock, closed her eyes, and waited.

A second voice replied to the first: "I can hear the river, so we must be close to it. Let's find it and follow it back to camp."

"Good idea!" said the first voice. "Which way is the river?"

"This way I think," said voice number two.

Something had been nagging at Isabel since the first voice came out of the fog. What was it?

That's it! The voices were speaking in *Spanish.* These must be soldiers from the Mexican army camp; they might know Alonso!

Isabel opened her mouth to ask, but the words dried up in her throat. She did not know if she could trust these men. And they would most certainly be suspicious of *her.*

Isabel made up her mind quickly. She would follow these men back to their camp. If it turned out to be the Mexican army camp, then she would announce herself and try to find Alonso. If it was not the army camp, then she could quietly slip away without anyone ever knowing that she was there.

So when two dark shapes shuffled past her rock toward the river, she silently followed.

# 22

The two men did belong to the Mexican army, and they did head for its camp on the banks of the Guadalupe.

Isabel hung back. She had had enough excitement and had no desire for more. She just wanted to find her brother, talk with him, and go home. That's all.

So she scouted the camp, trying to stay close enough to see but far enough away to avoid being seen herself. She had not seen Alonso yet, but she had only been there a short time.

The fog gave her a great sense of security and made her very, very happy. There would be no battle if people could not see to shoot at one another.

At least, that is what she believed until the first shots rang out.

People started running around and yelling. Shots seemed to be coming from all directions. Isabel heard horses whinny. A few more shots came from her left, then she heard someone cursing in a loud voice—a loud voice speaking *English.*

"Cease fire!" she heard from somewhere in front of where she had pressed herself against a tree.

"Fall back! Fall back!" said the same voice, a voice that was familiar to her. Who could it be? It took a moment, but then Isabel was able to match the voice to a face: Col. Moore from the Texas volunteers.

His surprise attack, it seemed, was a surprise to everyone—even him.

English-speaking voices faded off to her left, and Spanish-speaking voices talked excitedly to her right.

She was so busy trying to hear what was being said by both sides, that she failed to pay attention to what was going on closer to her. Isabel had crept out from behind her tree to hear more clearly, and she did not see the shadow that loomed up behind her.

But she did feel the blunt muzzle of a rifle when it poked into her back.

"Do not move," said a voice behind her.

Isabel had no intention of going anywhere.

"You are my prisoner," said the same voice.

Isabel nodded as the voice rose to a shout: "Lieutenant! Lieutenant! I have captured a spy!"

# 23

The Voice marched her through the mist to a big tent—the lieutenant's headquarters, she presumed. She stood there, outside the tent, waiting and not daring to turn around.

After half an hour or so, a tall, slim figure in a bright uniform brushed past her and disappeared into the tent.

It was another half hour before she was told to enter.

She felt the rifle jab her in the back again—softly once, then harder. So she moved quickly into the tent.

The person who had entered the tent earlier was sitting behind a table, writing something, and he did not look up for several moments.

"Well, Perez, and where is your spy?" he asked when he did finally stop writing.

"Right here, Lieutenant. Here is the spy," said the Voice.

"I am not a spy!" snapped Isabel to anyone who might care to listen.

"I found her emerging from behind a tree, just after all the shooting," said Perez.

"It seems to me that hiding behind a tree when there are shots being fired is an indication of great good sense, not proof of being a spy," said the man behind the table.

"Come here, girl " said the lieutenant. "What do you have to say for yourself?"

Isabel moved forward again at the prodding of the rifle. "I am not a spy," she said again.

"So you said the first time," replied the man. "Well if you're not a spy, little one, what are you? And what are you doing here in the middle of all this?"

Isabel was tired of people demanding answers from her. She wanted to refuse to answer this man. But she was tired, so very tired. And at this point, she just wanted to go home. She found herself telling the whole story, starting with how her brothers ran off. Tears ran down her cheeks as she told the lieutenant about her father getting shot.

She told him about finding Joaquin, only to be taken prisoner by his comrades. She told him about crossing the river and following his soldiers here. She concluded with a plea to see Alonso.

"My father is dying, sir, and my brother does not know it," she said. "Please let me see him."

The lieutenant was nodding by the time she finished.

"Perez," he said, looking past Isabel at the man who had captured her. "Go find young Alonso and tell him to report to me. Do not tell him what it is about."

"Yes sir!" said Perez. And he left.

By the time he returned, Isabel was sitting on the floor sipping water the lieutenant had given her.

Alonso followed Perez into the tent, and his eyes widened when he saw his sister.

"Isabel, what are you doing here?" he gasped.

Isabel flung herself at her brother and hugged him tightly.

"Father is dying, Alonso. You must come home," she said.

"What? How did this happen?" he exclaimed.

So Isabel told *him* the whole story, starting with the day he'd run off to join the army and ending with her capture by Perez.

By the time she finished, Isabel was slurring her words and her head was nodding in spite of her best efforts to stay awake.

"I think we need to let young Miss Isabel get some rest," said the lieutenant.

It was the last thing Isabel heard before succumbing to sleep.

# 24

Isabel awakened to the sound of a man cursing. She was curled up on a blanket in the corner of a tent, and the person who was swearing was standing outside.

"They broke their word! There was not supposed to be any fighting!" said a voice that Isabel recognized as the lieutenant's.

The officer stormed into his tent but pulled up short when he saw Isabel was awake.

"I am sorry to tell you that you are still a prisoner, as you might be able to tell the other camp something useful about us," he said. "You may leave when this situation is resolved. I must ask you not to leave this tent, but you will not be tied. In the meantime, I will send for your brother. I believe he has something to tell you."

\*\*\*

It was just as Isabel had known all along; politics definitely made people stupid. Alonso stopped briefly by the tent to tell her that he would not be returning home with her.

"I have made a commitment to a cause that is important," he said. "I cannot leave my comrades. I know father will understand. Please tell him this is my decision. He did not make me go. He is not responsible."

Then he was gone.

And the lieutenant left, too.

She heard him say, "So they want a fight? Fine. Let's see how they respond to our cavalry..." His voice faded as he got further away.

Alonso would not come home.

Joaquin would not come home.

Well I am going home, she thought. I am going home right NOW.

Nobody noticed as she slipped out of the tent and away from the camp. The fighting seemed to be coming from near the river, so she went the opposite direction.

Isabel heard a roar just as she reached the top of a little rise behind the camp. She turned and saw a thin white cloud of smoke drifting toward the Mexican troops. Shading her eyes from the sun, which had burned off the fog, she could see a cannon.

The men from Gonzales had dug up the cannon that the lieutenant had come to take. And they had used it against him.

Fluttering over it in the early morning breeze, Isabel could just make out a white flag with black letters on it: Come and Take It.

Isabel had made her decision. She was going home.

# 25

**S**ix hours later, she stumbled up the front porch steps of the big house at Rancho Montoya.

"Isabel! Oh Isabelina!" cried her mother. "Where have you been? What happened to you?"

But Isabel had no strength to tell her story again. She squeezed her mother's hand and then walked past her into the room where her father lay in bed.

Had he died while she was gone?

"Isabel? Is that you, my Isabelina?' Her Father's eyes fluttered opened. He lived!

She rushed to his bedside and dropped to her knees beside it.

"Father, I have chosen sides," she said.

"Oh no, *mija*, not you, too," he said.

"Yes, Father, I have."

Her father was shaking his head. "Well at least they will not let you into the army. Which side have you chosen?" he asked.

Isabel took a deep breath.

"I choose both and neither."

Her father looked puzzled. "But that is no side at all," he said.

"But it is," said Isabel. "It is the only side for us. I am Mexicano. I cannot change that. I do not want to change that. But I was born here in Tejas, so I am also a Texan. And if Texas becomes part of the United States someday, then I will be an

American. So I am for both and neither. That is what I choose. That is the Isabel side!"

Her father smiled.

"How did you get to be so wise, little one?" he asked.

Before she could reply, he said, "Very well then, I am for the Isabel side, too."

***

# The Real Story

## The Battle of Gonzales

The Battle of Gonzales was the first armed conflict of the Texas Revolution, but it really was not much of a fight at all. It was not even called a "battle" until many years later.

It all started when the Mexican government decided to take back a bronze cannon it had given the town of Gonzales in 1831 to help the people who lived there protect themselves against attacks by Native Americans.

There had been a revolt in Mexico, and the new government feared the Texans might start a revolution of their own. Officials from the new government decided it would certainly be silly if the Texans fought the Mexican government with a cannon the Mexican government had given them. So in September of 1835 the Mexican government asked the people of Gonzales to return the cannon.

This did not go over well with the Texans, who were already suspicious of the government. The people in Gonzales decided they would not give back the cannon. Instead, they hid it by burying it in a peach orchard.

Six Mexican soldiers arrived from the nearby town of San Antonio de Bexar (the town that is known today as San Antonio) to get the cannon. But instead of giving it to them, the people of Gonzales captured the men and escorted them out of town. The men were not thrown in the Guadalupe River; that only happened in *Messenger on the Battlefield*.

The military commander in San Antonio, a man named Col. Domingo Ugartechea, was not happy when he heard about this. He did not want to start a war, but he had to follow orders. If he did not get the cannon, then he would be in trouble.

So Col. Ugartechea sent Lt. Francisco Castaneda with about a hundred soldiers to get the cannon. He told Lt. Castaneda to do everything he could to avoid an armed conflict.

Just as in *Messenger on the Battlefield*, Lt. Castaneda and his troops arrived at Gonzales on September 29, 1835, but they could not get across the Guadalupe River. The residents had hidden the ferryboat in a bayou and taken all the other boats from that side of the river. And the waterway was impossible to cross without a boat at that point thanks to recent rainstorms, which had made it run fast and deep. So the Mexican soldiers could not cross.

On the other side of the river, eighteen Texans who lived in or near Gonzales were waiting for the Mexicans. They were ready to fight, even though they were outnumbered by more than four to one.

One of the Texans, a man named Albert Martin, told Lt. Castaneda that he must wait to cross until the town's mayor, called the alcalde, returned.

So that is what the Mexican troops did. They set up camp near the river on the highest ground they could find, a place called DeWitt's Mound. And they waited.

In the meantime, messengers from Gonzales were riding into the countryside and to nearby towns seeking volunteers. The eighteen men of Gonzales wanted others to come and help them fight. They were determined not to give the cannon back to the Mexican government.

Many men responded. They came from places such as Fayette and Columbus. By October 1, just two days after Lt. Castaneda arrived in Gonzales with his troops, the Texans outnumbered the Mexicans. Historians do not agree on how many men eventually fought on the Texans' side; the number was most likely between 140 and 190 men.

Back then, Texas armies elected their officers. So the men at Gonzales elected John Henry Moore from Fayette as their colonel, Washington Elliot Wallace from Columbus as lieutenant colonel, and Edward Burleson from Columbus as major.

Col. Moore called a meeting and asked the volunteers what they wanted to do. They decided they did not want to leave without fighting the Mexican troops.

Once that was decided, they got ready for battle.

Some men went to the peach orchard and dug up the cannon, while others found some old cart wheels for it. They knew that if the cannon had wheels, they could drag it along with them wherever they went.

They had no cannonballs, so some of the volunteers scrounged up scrap metal. They would put that in the cannon and fire it when the time came. Someone made a flag for the Texas troops. It was white and had a picture of a cannon on it and the words "Come and Take It."

On the other side of the river, Lt. Castaneda had learned that reinforcements had arrived to assist the original eighteen men of Gonzales. He decided to find a place where he could cross the river without a ferry, so he made his men march upriver looking for such a spot. They made camp on the night of October 1, 1835, about seven miles from where they were originally.

The same evening, the Texans put their ferry back in place and crossed the river in pursuit of the Mexicans. They marched all night, hoping to surprise the enemy. But in the early morning hours before the sun came up, they accidentally encountered the Mexican troops. Some shots were exchanged, but no one was hurt.

It was very foggy and no one could see to conduct a battle, so the commanders of both sides decided to wait until the sun came up to decide what to do.

It was October 2, 1835, and the first battle of the Texas Revolution was underway, although no one there at the time realized that.

When it got light, the Texans began shooting at the Mexicans, so Lt. Castaneda sent troops on horseback to attack them and the Texans retreated.

The two commanders, Col. Moore and Lt. Castaneda, met under a flag of truce to discuss the situation, but they could not work out a solution. Each returned to his own troops.

Col. Moore ordered his men to fire the cannon at the Mexican troops, then he led a charge against the enemy.

Lt. Castaneda had fewer men than the Texans and no cannon, so he retreated.

The Battle of Gonzales was over.

One soldier from Mexico's army had been killed. On the settlers' side, no one was killed, but there was one injury. A man was thrown from his horse and got a bloody nose when the Texans first encountered the Mexicans in the dark.

The Battle of Gonzales is sometimes called Texas's Battle of Lexington, a reference to the first official battle of the American Revolution when the "shot heard 'round the world" was fired.

### Dr. Launcelot Smither

Isabel and her entire family are fictional characters, but some of what happened to them in *Messenger on the Battlefield* really did transpire.

Isabel's experience of being captured by both sides during the Battle of Gonzales is based on the real life adventure of a fellow named Dr. Launcelot Smither.

The doctor lived in Gonzales in 1835. He was traveling and just happened to be in San Antonio de Bexar when the dispute over the cannon arose. Hoping to avert a battle, he went to visit Col. Ugartechea, the Mexican military commander. He wanted to end the conflict before anyone got hurt. The colonel agreed to let him be a go-between and promised that he would order his troops not to fire on the townspeople if the doctor could convince them to give up the cannon.

Dr. Smither agreed to deliver that message and speedily returned to Gonzales. Three Mexican soldiers accompanied him.

When they got back to Gonzales, the doctor reported to Lt. Castaneda, who asked him to take a message to the people of the town. He told the doctor that he just wanted to talk with whoever was in charge on the other side.

Dr. Smither delivered the lieutenant's message to an old acquaintance of his, someone he thought he could trust. He was told to spend the night in the Mexican camp since there would be no battle that night and to bring Lt. Castaneda to Gonzales with him on the following day. So that is what Dr. Smither did.

Not everyone had the same plans as Dr. Smither's friend, though. As it turned out, the rebels ended up attacking the Mexican soldiers that night. This made Lt. Castaneda very angry indeed. He thought Dr. Smither had deliberately lied and misled him to help the other side. So the lieutenant had the doctor put under arrest.

After more shooting between the two sides, Lt. Castaneda decided he needed someone who spoke English to deliver a message to the rebels. Dr. Smither was the perfect candidate. The lieutenant told him to try and set up a meeting with Col. Moore, the man who was commanding the Texas troops.

Dr. Smither was then released by the Mexicans, and he delivered the lieutenant's message to the rebels. But the Texans were suspicious of him, and Col. Moore arrested him.

So, because Dr. Smither got along with both sides, neither trusted him. Was he part of a plot to fool the Mexican troops or the Texans? Nobody knows.

### After the Battle of Gonzales

Other fights quickly followed the Battle of Gonzales, and the Texas Revolution was on. A doctor who lived in Gonzales remembered that many men flocked to Gonzales after hearing about the battle. "Some were for independence, some were for the Constitution of 1824, and some were for anything, just so long as it was a row."

After many fights, including the famous battle at the Alamo, Texans declared independence from Mexico in March of 1836. On April 21 of that year, the Texans led by Sam Houston defeated the Mexican army led by Santa Anna at San Jacinto.

Texas would be an independent republic for almost ten years before joining the United States as its twenty-eighth state in late 1845.

The eighteen men who first defied Mexican authority in Gonzales are now known as the "Old Eighteen." They are: William W. Arrington, Simeon Bateman, Valentine Bennet, Joseph D. Clements, Almon Cottle, Jacob C. Darst, George W. Davis, Almaron Dickinson, Graves Fulchar, Benjamin Fuqua, James B. Hinds, Thomas Jackson, Albert Martin, Charles Mason, Thomas R. Miller, John Sowell, Winslow Turner, and Ezekiel Williams.

Many of these men are mentioned in *Messenger on the Battlefield*. It is true that they were real people who were in Gonzales in September and October of 1835. And it is true that they defied the Mexican government and declined to give up the town's cannon. However, any other words or actions attributed to them in this story are fictional.

### The Town of Gonzales

The town of Gonzales was founded in 1825 as the capital of the DeWitt colony. Mr. Green C. DeWitt was a native of Missouri who had gotten a land grant and permission to settle 400 families there from the government of Mexico. He named his capital after Mexican patriot Rafael Gonzales, who was the Mexican governor of the area that included the colony.

*Green C. DeWitt, founder of Gonzales.*
Photo courtesy of Gonzales County Archives and Records Center, Gonzales, Texas.

The town was burned down twice—once by hostile Native Americans the year after it was founded and again in 1836 by Texas troops who were retreating from the Mexican army during the Texas Revolution.

In addition to the battle that now bears its name, Gonzales is famous for the thirty-two citizens who responded to calls for reinforcements at the Alamo. All thirty-two died there when the garrison fell. They are known as the "32 Immortals," and the Gonzales Memorial Museum is dedicated to them.

Among the displays at the museum is a cannon that some people claim is the one used at the Battle of Gonzales. However, this is unlikely. The cannon is made of iron, not bronze. According to some reports, the original bronze cannon from Gonzales was later used in the siege of San Antonio and then captured by the Mexican army and melted down.

Gonzales is also home to the only Confederate fort ever commissioned west of the Mississippi River. Its ruins can still be seen there today.

The town is about seventy miles east of San Antonio.

*"Come and Take It" flag and cannon at the Gonzales Memorial Museum, Gonzales, Texas.*

*Memorial to the "Old Eighteen" at the Gonzales Memorial Museum, Gonzales, Texas.*

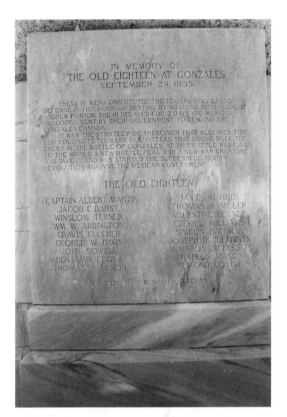

*Below: The Gonzales Memorial Museum, Gonzales, Texas*

*Memorial marking approximate site of the first shot fired in the Texas Revolution.*

*Below: Memorial near the site of the first battle of the Texas Revolution.*

### Mexican/Anglo relations

Many Mexican families lived in Texas long before Anglo colonists from the United States got permission to settle in the region. The two groups came seeking the same thing—opportunity. But they had a different language, different customs, and in most cases a different religion. These things conspired to keep the two groups mostly separate.

There were towns with intermingled populations—San Antonio and Nacogdoches, for instance. But those were the exceptions, not the rule.

When Texas finally revolted against Mexican rule, quite a few native Mexicans joined in on the side of the anti-government forces, just as Joaquin does in *Messenger on the Battlefield*. Though the Montoya family is fictional, their dilemma is something that many Mexicans faced in 1835 and 1836. The Texas Revolution made them choose between their pasts and their futures. Like Isabel, many struggled with the choice.

For them, the fiercest battles were not fought on the plains of Texas, but rather inside themselves.

# Sources

The Gonzales County Records Center and Archives

The Gonzales Memorial Museum (with special thanks to curator Mary Bea Arnold)

The Old Jail Museum in Gonzales, Texas

The Gonzales Chamber of Commerce and Agriculture , 414 St. Lawrence St., Gonzales, Texas 78629, 839-672-6532 www.gonzalestexas.com

Gonzales Pioneer Village Living History Center

*The Texas Revolutionary Experience: A Political and Social History 1835-1836* by Paul D. Lack (1992, Texas A&M University Press)

*Spanish Texas, 1519-1821* by Donald E. Chipman (1992, University of Texas Press)

*Battlefields of Texas* by Bill Groneman (1998, Republic of Texas Press)

*Texian Iliad: A Military History of the Texas Revolution, 1835-1836* by Stephen L. Hardin (1994, University of Texas Press)

*Hill Country* by Richard Zelade (1999, Lone Star Books)

*Lone Star: A History of Texas and the Texans* by T.R. Fehrenbach (1968 & 2000, Da Capo Press)

*The History of Texas (Second Edition)* by Robert A. Calvert and Arnoldo De León (1996, Harlan Davidson Inc.)

*A Browser s Book of Texas History* by Steven A. Jent (2000, Republic of Texas Press)

Texas State Historical Association

*Texans in Revolt – The Battle for San Antonio, 1835* by Alwyn Barr (1990, University of Texas Press)

*The New Handbook of Texas* edited by Ron Tyler, Douglas E. Barnett, Roy R. Barkley, Penelope C. Anderson and Mark F. Odintz (1996, The Texas State Historical Association)

Christy Storey of Broadway, North Carolina – special thanks for information about horses

# Other books in the Lone Star Heroines series

### Secrets in the Sky

It's1943 and the world is at war, but twelve-year-old Bethany Parker is stuck at home in Sweetwater, Texas. When the Women Airforce Service Pilots come to town, she is thrilled. They are glamorous and daring—and they befriend Bethany! When one of the women dies during a training flight, Bethany is convinced the mysterious crash was the work of a Nazi spy and she sets out to prove it.

### Fire on the Hillside

The spring of 1847 is approaching and Katherine Haufmann has just moved to Fredericksburg, Texas with her family from Germany. As she struggles to get used to her new home, thirteen-year-old Katherine becomes intrigued by the mysterious fires that start appearing in the nearby hills. While the rest of the town focuses on peace talks with the Comanche, Katherine decides to discover the cause of those fires.

# Other books in the Lone Star Heroes series

### Comanche Peace Pipe

Fish is eleven and on a wagon train headed west. Hunting Bear is a Comanche boy on his first war trail. When these sons of bitter enemies meet, there's suddenly danger all around. And all they can do is hang on for the wildest rides of their lives!

### On the Pecos Trail

Ride 'em cowboy! Eleven-year-old Fish and his best friend Gid set out to drive a herd of cattle to the Pecos River. Little do they know what excitement lies ahead. Stampedes, storms, even a twister—it's a trail they'll never forget!

### The Hidden Treasure of the Chisos

Only young Fish knows the way to lost gold in the Chisos Mountains. But a band of Apache wants it more than he does. Indians, ghosts, and animals gone mad—they're all waiting for him high in the Chisos crags!